Don't Let It Die Young

Whispers of Passion and the Shadows They Cast

BY SIMRAN YONZON

BLUEROSE PUBLISHERS
India | U.K.

Copyright © Simran Yonzon 2024

All rights reserved by author. No part of this publication may be reproduced, stored in a retrieval system or transmitted in any form or by any means, electronic, mechanical, photocopying, recording or otherwise, without the prior permission of the author. Although every precaution has been taken to verify the accuracy of the information contained herein, the publisher assume no responsibility for any errors or omissions. No liability is assumed for damages that may result from the use of information contained within.

BlueRose Publishers takes no responsibility for any damages, losses, or liabilities that may arise from the use or misuse of the information, products, or services provided in this publication.

For permissions requests or inquiries regarding this publication, please contact:

BLUEROSE PUBLISHERS
www.BlueRoseONE.com
info@bluerosepublishers.com
+91 8882 898 898
+4407342408967

ISBN: 978-93-6452-076-8

Cover design: Tahira
Typesetting: Tanya Raj Upadhyay

First Edition: August 2024

ACKNOWLEDGEMENT

First and most importantly, I would like to thank myself for always believing in myself even when times were rough and wild. There were people who told me that I would do nothing in life, but writing this book made me realize, I did it and I can do a lot of things in life even when I feel like giving up.

Aside from that, I would like to thank my family for sticking with me through thick and thin, especially my cousins. You have taught me how to stand on my own feet even when the whole world is upside down. I had seen that surviving in this real world also meant fighting through your struggles and playing a role to follow your dreams. Thank you for making me feel like my dream is worth it and yes, I would have definitely regret if I did not go ahead with this book. Hope is a strong word and yet the most powerful thing a person could ever pass on to another one.

To my remaining family members, I may not have mentioned each one of you but you all were equally there and I am forever grateful for that. I want to thank my two fathers, the one who is my birth parent and my father's brother who is more of a father to me than my father himself. (I am not mentioning your name for privacy concern and you both know who I am referring to). Life would not be easy without you both.

The man with Gabriel tattoo, despite this book being complete fiction, all your characteristics are real. Your identity maybe unknown and I will leave your identity anonymous. Thank you for keeping me focused and making me feel like I should go ahead with my work.

Last but not the least, I want to thank the professional team who helped me with publishing this book and my dear readers, thank you for bringing out the woman that I am in me. I can proudly call myself, "The Author" now. Thank you for the support.

INTRODUCTION

Elizabeth, a weaver of words, lived for the symphony of sentences and the solace of stories. But her world lacked a face, a muse to ignite the embers of inspiration. Then, fate, a fickle artist itself, crossed her path with Henry. With a sculpted face that defied cameras and eyes that held galaxies, he wasn't just a model, he was a living sculpture, a breath-taking contradiction of stoic grace and smoldering intensity.

For Elizabeth, he became the missing verse, the melody that set her soul to music. Every glance, every stolen moment, fueled the inferno of her creativity. But love, like a sculptor's chisel, can chip away at even the most stoic exteriors. Was Henry content to be her eternal muse, a figment of her literary fancy, or did his heart yearn for something more real, a love that transcended the pages of her fantastical worlds?

This is their story, a love letter penned in stolen moments, whispered desires, and the unyielding pursuit of dreams. Can their love bridge the chasm between fiction and reality, or will the weight of expectation shatter the fragile edifice of their happily ever after?

CHAPTER 1

Heavy breathing, slow touches. He pushes me to the wall, strips my beautiful golden satin gown, unhooks my bra, unlaces my thong and within few seconds, I am naked in front of him. He gently grabs my hand, turns me around and starts to fuck me.

"Henry Walker, be gentle I say," moaning so loud that all 32 rooms in his large house could hear me or at-least I thought they heard me. The aesthetics of his room often make me feel like I am some princess being fucked by the prince. It felt royal.

"Don't worry darling, I've asked all my maids to take a day off," he says.

He then carries me to his bed, and starts kissing me. All I can hear was him breathing and I could not control any longer. I wanted him to fuck me like I'm his and he is mine. He starts licking my body downwards and starts eating me. I was holding his head, careless about what's next. I start moaning louder and louder, he kisses me while fingering me. Of course, I was hornier than he was at that point.

He gently licks me and inserts two fingers inside me. I wanted to be his and only his so I was letting him dominate me. He inserts one more finger inside me, I can't express how I felt. It was so deep and the orgasms were too good to be true. Henry can be a highly pleasurable man, I must say.

While teasing and playing during sex, I was focused on his tattoo. He had tattooed the arch angel Gabriel on his arm and several small tattoos on both of his hands, total of 9 tattoos.

He looks at me and smiles.

I ask him, "What are you looking at?"

He says, "Your eyes!! It makes me want to go missionary, it's pretty."

I blush and start kissing him. He started fucking me missionary while we made love. His eyes are light brown, the same as mine and that was the best birthday sex, I ever had with him.

And of course, it was my birthday, stupid 24 years ended with crazy sex.

Henry and I, were attracted to each other from the first time we met at the school library. We were both searching for the same book at the library since we both loved reading. As there was only one, we shared the book and made few conversations until we had to leave, so we planned on adding each other on social media.

He is a gym freak and is an introvert except for when it comes to me. His hair is soft and he likes keeping his medium mullet style. He is 6'2 and he is good at every sport he plays, especially basketball. He is the typical "IT" boy. He had and has a lot of options but he keeps choosing me over and over again. At the age of 18, he started his career as fitness model. Not to mention, his 30th birthday was coming soon.

As for me, I am an ambivert. I am 5' with long straight hair and thick who has hour glass figure and blonde hair. I am a writer and I am very proud what I am.

We both are quite opposites; I am generally not good at expressing my feelings while he loves me loud and clear. We share our fair share of ups and downs. We have our bad days and good days. We fight and we keep coming back to each other. But we, we stay loyal and stick to each other.

Apart from our love for books, we loved travelling with each other and trying new foods. He is a typical London boy with a sexy British accent and I, have American accent being American, who chose to follow her dreams and leave everything behind. Our first meet being at the library in America, we stayed in touch through social media until I shifted to London for my career.

It has been one year, eight months in London and I must say, that fate is indeed beautiful.

He often reads me books at night and tells me stories about how his day was. Drives me to work and picks me up from work.

Henry is the kind of man; you would want to write books about and here I am, writing a book about him. I, Elizabeth Carter, am madly in love with this man. He makes me explore the versions of myself that I have yet to discover and always got me doing things that makes me happy. He loves the versions of me that I don't let anybody see and we are bound together like stars. If all of the pieces in a puzzle could fall into pieces without missing a single piece, it would be us. Even if something as vast and scattered as the stars were to fall apart, every piece would come together to form "us."

He is **charismatic**.

CHAPTER 2

On my birthday, I wake up with a letter beside me.

"Hey Beautiful,

Wake up with a smile on your face, we are doing something new today.

Meet me for lunch at 14 Hills. Located on the 14th floor of a Fenchurch Street skyscraper.

-Your boyfriend"

I rushed to get ready after reading. And as you read earlier, Henry strips my gown. I was definitely wearing the same gown. He was in awe when he looked at me. Our friends, cousins and Henry were waiting at 14 Hills with some presents for me. He gifts me a kitten and after some serious conversation, we name her Bella. She is one of the most gorgeous Persian cats I have ever had. Grey fur and pretty eyes.

As my brother suggested we start eating instead of chit chatting, we started focusing on the food.

Oh!! How I love his choice of food. I focused more on eating Halibut and Beef Fillet. He was fidgeting with his Chateaubriand.

I ask him, "What's up?"

He says, "How about we go back to my house and fuck?"

I blushed and asked him to shut up.

After long hours of talking and lunch, the waiter brings out my birthday cake.

As pink is my favorite color and he ordered a pink cake with a message, "Happy 24 Love."

Living never lost its magic, I must say. A day well spent. You are already aware of what happened after we went back home. Let me tell you about the next day.

We both woke up around 11:30AM, I can hear Bella cry. She is way too soft and I start ordering food for her while looking at her tiny paw. Being a cat mother, it is my first and I wanted to be at my best.

While Henry asked his maids to switch one of his rooms into a playroom for Bella, I prepared some food for her. We went to shop for Bella, and we ended up getting too many toys but all in pink. We got a flower shaped cat tree and a house shaped bed in pink, again. After decorating the room, we see Bella sleeping peacefully and purring.

We were too tired so we asked maids to cook some Indian food. During dinner, as we were eating Chicken curry and rice along with some other vegetables. I asked Henry if I could stay at my own apartment in Notting Hill for few days as I wanted to focus on writing my book.

He denied, and stated that it is too far from his house knowing that Knightsbridge and Notting Hill are not far. I take a deep breath and tell him, it's not that far.

He says, "Am I not clear? You are going nowhere!! You can take all of these rooms and write hundreds of books, but there is no way I'm letting you go there. I give zero fuck about how you feel about going to that apartment, I'll never allow. And you should leave the apartment too."

"You must be sick or something, why would I leave my apartment because of your petty jealousy" I state.

I stand up and go to our bedroom to avoid arguments as I always hated arguing with him.

Henry really has some problem with David Stevens, my neighbor. I met David when I had just shifted to London and I was not dating Henry back then. Coincidentally, we used to meet every morning while jogging and one of the days, I twisted my ankle so helped me. While sitting on the bench at the park where we used to jog, we asked each other where we were originally from and shared some stories about US. He told me he visits US often. While heading back home together, we got to know that we were neighbors too. He has this beautiful house right opposite to my apartment. You could make out that David was rich just by looking at him and the clothes he wore. He invited me to parties several times, and I met his friends too. He looked like a man with class and rich taste.

Later, I found out that he is the Chairman of the company where I work, while making a presentation for events. So, I tried to maintain my distance until I met him at office party where my boss, Katy introduced us officially and David started questioning me why I was avoiding him. When I told him the reason, he laughed it off and told me to think of him as a friend since we met before we knew he would be the boss of my boss.

Let me get back to this later.

For all that Henry should know, we have a bond that remains whole despite fragmentation. I would keep choosing him.

CHAPTER 3

I was sleeping on the bed; Henry tucks me in properly. After I walked out from dinner, he came to sleep in late. He gently whispers, "it is not because of my jealousy. I cannot see you staying away from me even if it for few minutes". He gets inside the blanket and turns to the other side to sleep. I turn around to his side, gently touch his arm. He turns to my side and says that he does not want to fight.

"Neither do I", I said.

He starts kissing me gently and rubs his hand on my breasts. I can't say I felt nothing. He pulls me and put me on top of him, still kissing gently. He stops and stares at me then kisses me again. He unlaces my thong, and slides his penis inside me. I am still wearing my baby doll while riding him, he grabs my ass and we are kissing. He turns me around and starts to fuck me from behind. He was going slow, because slow sex makes me want him more.

While the intercourse was slow from behind, he was holding my thighs. He then runs his fingers slow, while I am still in the dog position. He pulls out his penis, slides 3 fingers inside me and start to use his tongue. It was that moment I knew I was going to get fucked. I was wet and wanted to be submissive to him. Henry knew how to use his tongue and make love. He knew what he was doing.

He tears my baby doll, that I had just bought and tells me that he will buy as many as I want later. We were laughing and kissing. He comes on top of me, slides his penis inside me and takes it rough. Holding my neck and once again I am on top of him. He spanks me harder as I ride him. He goes down on me and then I perform oral sex. I start slow, using my hand, playing and licking him. Exploring the rhythms and pressure, using my mouth and tongue. We were done after some hours.

We then quickly head to shower together. The water was cold and the night was long. We quickly fell asleep.

Next morning, we woke up cheerful. I mean who would not.

He was getting ready for gym and I had to join too. We both hit the gym together. Ever since I dated Henry, I had stopped going out for jogging, since we often slept late and jogging wouldn't be fun if it is not early morning. Bodyspace, is a private wellness club and since Henry is a fitness model with taste, he preferred the luxurious and private space there. He is a proud man and can sometimes become difficult for me to keep up with his routine.

After gym, we showered together and I was joining him for his photoshoot. It made me proud and happy to see him invested in himself and he loved his career. Once the shoot was over, we both had to definitely go for shopping as we were leaving for Paris soon to celebrate his birthday. Henry wanted to spend his day, only with me.

Harrods and The Royal Exchange, I must say, are the only malls where he goes for shopping. Henry does not settle for anything else when it comes to shopping for clothes. I just love his old money outfits, even though I prefer him shirtless. I love gazing at his abs and I love how shredded he is. The man that most woman can dream of.

I can give a list of things I love about him. The way he holds the door open for me every time and the way he pulls out the chair for me to sit. It is bare minimum for a gentleman but for this generation, it is something that a woman can only ask for. He cooks food for me, gets me sanitary napkins every time I'm ovulating, does shopping for me and most of the times, even do my laundry. I hardly lift my hand for house chores as he treats me like I am delicate.

Even though we fight, I would die for this man. People always talk about the ones that make them feel butterflies or heartache. I get butterflies every time he looks at me and smiles. His dimples make me want him and need him more. While my heartaches, every time we are far from each other, busy with our own family and work.

Speaking of family, let me tell you about our family.

CHAPTER 4

I understand, everyone has a past. Every family got story to tell. Well, both of our family certainly does too.

Henry was always loved by his mother and he is truly his mother's son. Isabella got married at a very young age and later, due to miscarriage she lost her first child. After a year, she was pregnant with Henry. Henry was 12 years old when he lost his father, Nathan died due to a car accident. He surely misses his father and he has promised to look after his mother ever since. As his father passed away due to the accident, Henry was the owner of Real Estate business and twelve family vacation homes that his father owned which was being handled by his mother as he had no interest in his family business, even though he had to take over it one day. His father loved cars and Henry inherited several cars including Rolls-Royce Phantom, David Brown Automotive Speedback GT, Bugatti Chiron and Ferrari Enzo. Me being big fan of cars, it left me in awe when I visited his house for the very first time. Henry often drives me to work in his Royce Phantom or Bugatti Chiron since I love them.

I often meet Isabella when she is visiting London or when we visit New York. Once Henry turned 18, she shifted to New York permanently since New York reminds her of her late husband and their honeymoon.

They were high school sweethearts and she often mentioned that she felt empty without her husband. She was unable to fill that void in her life.

I remember the day I met her.

Harry and I, were just casually talking to each other and going out on dates back then because we both were not ready to be in a relationship yet and he never told me how he felt about me. It had been three months since I shifted to London. I used to meet David on regular basis because I am working for his company. While I was waiting for the car outside the office, David stopped his car and asked me to visit The Arts Club in London to see the exhibition along with him. I couldn't say no and I was little interested to know about the art.

David said, "I have taken a membership for you here, you can come and take inspiration anytime you want."

As he explained Reginald Sylvester II: Feelin' Blue to me (the art). I was focused on his face. He is hot, I wouldn't lie.

I turned around to see Henry standing. He walked up to me and said, "What are you doing here? And who is this gentleman?" in his perfect British accent.

David interrupted me by saying, "I am David Stevens, her formal boss and her friend."

Having no reason, Henry was rude to him and said, "Did I ask you?"

I say, "David and I, we are friends, we met several times before I got to know he is the owner of the company I work in."

All he could hear was several times, he sighs out loud, "Several times, I get it."

"Enjoy!!" – he said and left.

I was clueless of what happened, I told David not to mind Henry being rude to him.

I went back to my apartment, freshened up and was about to fall asleep at 11pm. I got a call from Henry. As soon as I received the call, he asked me if I was still out with David. I told him that I was back at my apartment and I went there only for work.

He questions me – "What about meeting several times?"

I ask him to chill. I tell him about how I met David and there is nothing going on between both of us. He does not believe it and he asked me if he could come over and meet me.

He came over and started asking me about David again. I tell him that he cannot keep questioning me because we are not in a relationship.

He says, "What if I tell you that I want a future with you and I cannot see you with someone else?"

I stay silent and he shouts, "What the fuck! Say something!"

I tell him how absurd it is for him to ask me to be in a relation with him just because of his petty jealousy. He grabbed my hand and started kissing me and it was my first kiss. I stopped him and he asked me if I am free the next day. He asked me to change my clothes and head out with him as soon as he heard that I had no work the next day.

I wear a backless satin top and mini skirt in pink, we go out to grab some food as he was hungry. He asks me to stay with him for the night and he will behave well. I am a bloody fool to believe that he would behave. It was the first time I saw his house and I was amazed. Let me tell you, it looks like a palace. We went out on several dates and spoke on calls, but it was for the first time he took me to his house and told me about his family. It was also the first time I let a man, I like, to come into my apartment and my first kiss. Conversations after conversations, he comes to the bed from the chair and sits near me, I was scared and I thought he will behave, he started kissing me. As he leans on me, I went back laying my head on the pillow. He held my hand and kissed me. We were cuddling on bed; he slowly touched my Inner thigh which is my weak point and then he slowly slides his hand inside my panty and circles his finger around my clit.

Now, if you are reading this, I know you are labelling me as a slut because who sleeps with a man at the very first day you get in a relation. But I did and it was my first. Henry is the person who took away my virginity.

As he touched me, I started getting butterflies and we had sex. He was slow and he paid attention to every single scar on my body. Even when I think about us having sex, he got me touching on my body.

Next morning, I met his mother. I had just woken up and I was at the living room which is his entire ground floor. The bell rang and I opened the door. She was crying and she looked too young for me to believe that she is his mother. I told her Henry was sleeping and she asked me not to wake him up. It was my first time meeting my boyfriend's mother and she found me wearing a t-shirt and his shorts. She understood the rest.

She asked me, "Are you dating my son?"

I nod.

She gave a cheerful smile and forgot about her problem and started telling me how she met his father, got married, had miscarriage, gave birth to Henry and lost her husband. Henry woke up in meantime and joined us.

At night I heard some voices and Henry telling his mother that he should stay away from his father's brother, Lando who was eyeing on their properties.

And as the saying goes, there is always a snake in every family. His father died in car accident because of his uncle who crashed his car after getting drunk. Henry and his mother always stayed away from him as they could not bring themselves to like him or be around him.

Some humans are just pathetic and love living in misery.

CHAPTER 5

I am holding on to every single memory that is dead and gone. Even though I can't love people right sometimes. I'm more trouble than I am worth at times. We often say we are fine; we are still a liar. Sometimes the pain hurts so good, we can't let go. I tell people I am fine, but it is complicated. So complicated. I used to be wide awake at night for years and try to reach for a hand only to find myself drowning.

Family? Yes, I have a complicated family. Who knew parents can break you more than any person you love could? I am not catastrophizing but I am impatient and overthinking, all because my mother broke my heart into so many pieces that no one can ever fix it.

A child needs someone to hold on to them. A child needs love, attention and care. A child needs peace and happy memories. A child needs both their parents. When I was a child, I had to mature quickly. I got to know, my parents aren't heroes, my parents are normal humans. I bottled up my emotions so much that I felt suffocated. Now, I cannot express my love and affection unless I am writing.

I used to shut my door and listen to music to avoid listening to my parents fight. I used to be mad when they acted like a normal family like nothing was wrong. My mother, Olivia cheated on my father, Lucas when I was still in school. I was young but old enough to understand what was wrong. They tried adjusting for years, fighting and arguing just to make sure that I have both my parents. Until my mother decided to leave.

But the fact that neither one of them were right, I cannot really blame her. My father loved her so much that he chose to stay with her despite her cheating on him and taking more than half of his money and properties just to feed her boyfriend's need. And the fact my mother cheated on my father was not wrong enough, she gave my brother and my custody to my father in exchange for his luxury clothing business and his love for his daughter, made him make the sacrifice that has been being passed on family for generations.

Money gets you a lot of things, and the very same thing made him lose his lover and keep his daughter and son. I applaud my father for the sacrifices he made. I always hold him close to my heart. It is funny how I disliked my mother. Despite the business he lost, he owned many hotels in America, so his business was thriving. My elder brother who is two years elder than Henry, is named William. William was always protective about me and loved me in ways that my mother never did. I was only seven years when William was fourteen years old and our parents got divorced. He took responsibilities for me when my father was not recovering from heartbreak.

Three years later, when my father had already moved on, my mother came back to our life asking for forgiveness. Apparently, her lover left her for someone else. As it should be, cheaters get cheated on. She was now an alcoholic and penniless. Even so, my father helped her to get in rehab and never looked back. He had simply moved on.

That is something, he did right. I pity my mother but she is just reaping her Karma. I do not hate her, I don't. Sometimes, life has different purpose and they were simply not meant for each other. But I despise the fact that she gave birth to me and chose money and a new lover over family.

My father always treated me like a delicate flower and used to tell me stories. He never denied for things that I wanted. My brother used to call me a spoiled brat but he used to spoil me much more than my father did. He sneaked ice-creams at night just because I crave for ice-creams at night and gets clothes for me every single time he travelled.

Love? I was loved right but somehow my mother broke all three of us in the process of seeking for her own kind of love. I was holding on too tight for my mother's love but how could I love and trust her again.

My boyfriend loves being around my father and for some reasons, my father pays more attention to what Henry loves more than mine. I won't lie by saying I do not get jealous. My brother always teases me when I get jealous about that but I know they would not trade the world for me.

It's funny how they met for the first time, I clearly remember the day after I met Isabella for the first time, I went back to my apartment and I was having a mild fever. I hadn't called my family for five days and couldn't receive calls either so they assumed something happened. Henry was taking care of me, when the doorbell rang and he went to open it, he saw my father and brother standing with a worried look on their face.

My father assumed something must have had happened so they rushed to meet me. Isabella was also in my apartment.

"Who are you? Where is my daughter? What are you doing here?" - With shock my father questioned him.

"If you are referring to Elizabeth, she is sleeping" - Henry replied.

I could hear my brother shouting at Henry, "What do you mean by sleeping? Did you both sleep?"

By the time Isabella rushed out to see what was happening outside. Henry replied, "She is sick and we are looking after her. She is my girlfriend and yes, we did sleep together."

Isabella controlled the noise by saying that all three of us slept together for few days since I was not well; I could hear murmurs coming from the hall. My father and Isabella were introducing each other and getting to know about Henry and me. While my brother was asking Henry to stop sleeping with me and be good to me. I stood up from bed and went to see them. I could see that my father was concerned about me.

My brother said, 'Thought you wouldn't wake up at all."

Henry understood and changed the topic by telling my father that I have been working extremely hard and won best writer award for the year. Isabella called everyone for lunch and everyone left to join. My father asked me about my relationship with Henry.

I told him that Henry makes me happy.

My father smiled and started talking to Isabella. They both had been single for so long and they found someone of their age to share stories with. I looked at Henry and smiled. He stood from the chair he was sitting on and came to sit beside me.

Once lunch was over, my brother came to my room and asked me if I really slept with Henry, I smiled and said, he is a good guy.

"Know your limits" – William said and went to play basketball with Henry.

They had become really close while I was recovering and now, year later, they are on good page. I feel like my father trusts Henry more than me sometimes.

He got me riding on the palm of his hand and all I see is him. I rather him walk over me than walk away.

CHAPTER 6

Dreams do come true.

We were here to celebrate Henry's 30th birthday at Paris. My dream city, city of love, city of fashion and city of happiness. It was very late when we reached, so we checked in at **Hotel de Crillon**, my favorite place to be. I had always heard about it. It was my first time in this city, where I always wanted to live and find love. But I was here with my love. We were pretty tired to go anywhere so we slept.

Next morning, we wake up with energy and passion. Henry was cuddling me from behind, I believe both of us have a high sex drive. He pulls me closer to him, opens my thong and toss it on the floor. He throws his brief on the floor and was naked, cuddling with me. He starts breathing on my neck and starts licking my ear.

He runs through me like bad drugs and I am addicted. He knows my weakness and keeps playing with it. He rubs my inner thigh with his hand. His big arm is holding me close to him. He then puts my fingers inside his mouth, spits on it and makes me touch myself down there. I am facing him and he is facing me, while his hand is holding my hand and I am touching myself.

He winks at me and gives a smile, that million-dollar smile. Out of all the art in museums, he is an art, that got me hooked. No matter how many different arts I get to see, I will never be able to erase the perfection of this art from my vision. His dimples crave imprints of happiness and can steal all the thunder of diamonds. Mr. Gabriel tattoo is perfection. I slowly remove my hand from myself and touch his abs, damn, his abs are hard and he got eight packs.

He kisses me on my forehead and says, "Get ready, we will have a little tour."

We got ready for Paris tour and went to Starbucks first, I ordered my regular Choco Chip Frappe Grande and he ordered his Vanilla Expresso and also some food for takeaway in case I would want to hog food. We went to the Louvre Museum, Luxembourg Garden and other places for sightseeing and later evening, we went to see only the Eiffel Tower and had dinner in one of the restaurants there and I had secretly made a reservation for his birthday there.

After dinner, one of the servers brought his birthday cake out and I said, "Happy 30th birthday, Love." With a kiss on his cheeks, I gave him Louis Vuitton Pharrell jacket which I had secretly arranged as well. He was filled with joy.

We went back to the hotel, tired and sleepy. As soon as we got inside the bed, we dozed off.

The entire week was followed by visiting places in Paris, trying new food and doing hell lot of shopping. A week well spent with the love of your life is a must.

Too much laughter and happiness, bring too much attention and thunder. While we had fun and good times, we had chaos and heartbreak waiting for us. I too have started believing in the evil eye concept. When you are so in love and people see you happy, misery follows. It was time to go back, get to work and have a hectic work life.

We went back to our daily routine. Apart from gym, we met straight at night on the bed. After sex, we went to sleep for couple of days. As you know our intimacy is always on point, but I used to be too tired to even move sometimes so we used to just cuddle and get some sleep.

I was almost at the peak of my career with so much responsibilities and I had to often hangout with David due to work. We had to visit museums and other places together to get inspiration for the work. Henry, of course he was not happy about it but he kept holding onto his insecurities and kept bottling things up. He suddenly started acting distant, not because of work but because I was always busy with David. He felt left out.

I had many projects to finish, and it was late. So, David invited me to his house to finish the pending work. I dropped a message to Henry mentioning that I am at work with David and I will be late. I knew he would not be happy to know that I am at his house so I did not tell him. While working on the project, we were painting some models for book ideas and I dropped the paint water on me. I was wearing a white see-through fur dress with a lace black bralette. David quickly helped me with napkin yet I got the paint water all over my dress. He offered some change of clothes; I wore his tee-shirt and shorts since I had nothing else to wear. We continued our work and I left.

Henry was fast asleep when I reached. I asked the maid to help me wash my dress and went to change, as I was about to change, Henry stormed in the other washroom and asked me what was I wearing. I was forced to tell him what happened, he was a bit insecure.

He says, "Wow!! Thought you would not wear any other man's clothes"

I reply, "What is that supposed to mean?"

"Nothing." – he says and left.

When I went to bed, Henry did not look at me once or cuddle with me.

Thought he would be over it by next morning but he started acting cold towards me. I assumed he needed some space so I did not disturb him for some time. I got busy with my work and the routine with Henry went the same, cold and distant.

CHAPTER 7

Work pressure had no time for me to get some personal time with Henry and he too was distancing himself from me. He assumed all the things that he shouldn't have. Me being myself, I assumed that he would get over it soon. It has been two months since I missed my periods. I was scared about the worst and I thought of getting a pregnancy test before telling Henry. I bought some test kits and after getting a positive response, I took a doctor's appointment. I was quite terrified to know that I am actually pregnant and before I could actually decide whether I should keep the baby or not, I decided to let Henry know about it. Because I knew he would support me for whatever decision I would take.

That night I went home early and right after meeting the doctor. I was happy to think about starting a new life and I was worried how our parents would react. I was worried if Henry was ready to be a father. Henry came home late and drunk. Before I could say anything, he accused me of sleeping with David, my boss. He knew that I loved him and I would never do anything but after listening to his friend, Shelly's opinion, he became quite negative towards me.

Drunk Henry told me, "I know you slept with David, Shelly told me that is what woman do when they are tired of dating someone. They stay away and distant and fuck their boss."

Without thinking a second thought, I slapped him and left him alone.

After overthinking for the whole night, I was packing my belongings the next morning to leave him. I had to be ready for what my future holds and ready for the thought or having a baby or not. Life is not perfect after all. He was the greenest flag a man could ever be but how could he be manipulated for something so petty without knowing what was going on in my life. I know life would be no fairytales but I actually thought we would trust each other despite what was going on in my life.

Henry comes to the room to apologize and says that he should not have listened. I calmly tell him that I am leaving because the accusations were pointing fingers at my character. It was like he knows me so well but still chooses the fact of becoming far from me. He was old enough not to jump into conclusions because of someone else's opinion.

I guess every relation hits the rock bottom and love falls apart for petty reasons. I carried my luggage and left from my room, still arguing with Henry. He told me that he got manipulated and when he tried to stop me, I was standing on the stairs, he pulled me back but I still tripped and fell down along with him. We were fine after falling down so I thought it did not make any difference.

But I started feeling quite uneasy in the uber and asked the driver to drop me to my apartment quickly. The uneasy feeling increased. I was 12 weeks pregnant so I knew something was not right. Knowing I had no one to call during emergency, since my family lived miles away. I called Henry again, in tears.

"Hello!! Are you ready to talk now?" - Henry said.

Sobbing to tears because of the pain, I say - "I am feeling uneasy, I need to go to doctor."

"Book the uber now and rush to the hospital, I am on my way." - He said.

I quickly booked the uber and met him at the hospital. The doctor ran some tests on me and Henry was looking at me with big eyes with no idea of what was going on since I had no time to update him. The doctor took him out of the room to speak with him. I was looking at their expressions through the glass and it definitely didn't not seem much of good news. Henry came inside the room and hugged me.

I told him - "What did she tell you?"

He says with a sad face - "You know life is not always perfect and sometimes we lose things we want the most. Please do not panic. And hear me out, you had a heavy bleeding and most of the tissues had passed by the time you visited the doctor. The cramping and pain in your lower tummy and the discharge of fluid and tissues, were the signs of having a miscarriage. This may feel like the end to it, but it is not. You still have me. You can cry and let your heart out if you want to."

All the dreams and imagination shatters. The little life I had longed for shatters. I break into tears of physical, mental and emotional pain.

I knew it was no one's fault except mine when I fell down, but somehow, I wanted to blame someone and I think I blamed Henry for that.

He was there for me and loved me. I knew for a matter of fact that he was the only person who would ever love me this way, but I chose distance over the fact of discussing this and letting my heart out would be my closure.

I flew back to my parents without telling him anything. This was not the end of us, but I wanted to be away from him and away from my life.

CHAPTER 8

I was in America, back with my family. I was doing nothing apart from existing and breathing. My father was forcing me to eat food, but I was still grieving, so I was not in a mood to do anything apart from being restless. They knew nothing about what was going on. All they knew was that I had taken off from my work and I went back home. My father, being a father, knew something was not right, and he spoke to Henry since I was not reacting to anything. I still do not have any idea of what Henry told my family about us and what happened.

Henry kept trying to contact me, but I needed some space, so I ignored all his calls. Before I knew anything, months passed by, and I was just taking a long break doing absolutely nothing. One day, David suddenly called me and asked me if I would actually come back to work as they needed me. I knew it was time for me to get back to my work and focus on my career as I had taken a long break. A break long enough for anyone to be fired. Grieving for your loss and pain does not give an excuse for you to quit your work. This is the reality and I had to wake up and snap back to work.

Henry tried to contact me for a month, and he too gave up on calling me. He had come to America to meet me, but I hung up on him. He had to leave, and maybe he understood that I needed space and I needed time.

Life is fun until it falls apart and shatters. You cannot deny the fact that life goes on with or without. I used to stay home and miss Henry's voice, touch, smile and slow breathing. It is the fact, I used to miss him a lot. But when you are in pain, you blame someone and he was my escape. I kept thinking that had he not doubted me with David, had he not argued with me or tried to stop me, we would have been fine. The baby would have been fine.

That morning, I was leaving because I was angry that he could get manipulated easily and think so little about the love I have for him. I did not leave because I wanted to stay away from him. I did not leave because I thought that the baby did not need a father. I knew that the baby would need a father. I was also angry that I could not tell him that I was pregnant, and I assumed that telling him would make him think it was David's child, since he was already thinking that I was fucking around.

I was scared of raising the child alone. But I knew that I would tell him when the time would actually be right for us. I would tell him when I am not angry at him anymore. But little did I know he would hear about my miscarriage before he would ever hear about my pregnancy. Never did I know the start would be the end as well. I was going through a lot of emotions and I really needed a long break. I had no idea how Henry was coping with it or what was happening. I missed him a lot. I spent my time crying to myself. I would rather die than live without this man. It was only the space I wanted because I had a void in me. The void that needed closure.

Out of many lessons I learned in life, I learned to be honest with him even if that meant little arguments and fights. Out of many chapters of my life, this CHAPTER was meant for healing and learning. This CHAPTER left a big scar on me, but it also made me realize how I could not live without him.

Henry surely loves me more than I love him. But he focuses on words along with actions. I knew taking some time away from him really hurt him deep down. After all, we both lost the baby. I was not alone. He did too.

I knew that the baby meant something to him as well, even though he had no idea about the child that was growing inside me. I knew that he was in pain as well and my actions had hurt him. I picked myself pieces by pieces, but I wondered if he was fine.

I called Henry and he quickly picked up. I told him that I was coming back to London, and we needed to talk.

I packed, and before I left for London, I went to my father's room and told him that I needed to get back to work, so I was leaving. I think my father understood that I needed a break from reality when life falls apart, so he was quite happy when I said I needed to get back to work.

I knew he was not happy to see me sitting idle and not talking to anyone. But he gave me the space and time I needed, and for that I am grateful.

Before I left, my father told me to check up on Henry.

I know this is a scar that will live on me forever, but we both have lives ahead of us.

I reached London at four in the morning and went straight to Henry's house.

CHAPTER 9

As soon as I arrived, I rang the doorbell and Shelly, the woman I do not like at all, opened the door for me. Shelly started arguing with me in the lobby.

She clearly said, "You know that I think Henry would be better without you. You have hurt him enough, and he surely deserves a better woman in his life. I have liked him for the longest time and I would treat him much better than you did."

I told her - "Wow! You certainly know how to manipulate someone and for God's sake, stop trying to meddle in our lives."

She says - "He slept with me multiple times and told me that I am good in bed."

My heart shattered again so I slapped her and Henry came downstairs rushing to see what was going on. Shelly starts crying and tells Henry that I slapped her and started accusing her of sleeping with him. Henry looks at me and asks what was going on.

I tell him that they deserve each other, and she was manipulating him again, and he is a fool to get manipulated again. I was so angry and in pain that I would have slapped him too.

He hugs me and says – "It's okay. Calm down and I trust you."

Then he looks at Shelly and asks her to leave if she was here to create a fight not there with him as a friend.

I asked him if he really slept with her. He denies. It was a relief for my ears.

Another lesson for your love life: What you see is not always real. What you hear is not always the truth. And what you feel is not always right. Sometimes you need to confront your partner rather than assuming or listening to a third person. Life is not always black and white; you never know who is actually your friend or your enemy.

I was tired from traveling and the drama, so he asked me to rest and we would talk later. He met me after so long, and he did not want to leave me for a second. I was still in pain, and he could understand that, so we went to bed just holding each other's hands. I slept for more than ten hours, and he did not have work. He was lying in bed thinking hard about what was bothering him. When I opened my eyes, he was looking at me. His eyes were focused, so I panicked and closed my eyes again.

He smirked and said, "It's nearly evening. Don't you want to eat?"

I said – "I am hungry, but I need to talk to you first."

He suddenly became serious, and I started my conversation with the word, 'sorry'. I told him how I felt and why the distance was necessary. He was mature enough to understand what I was going through, and he did not deny or say anything else apart from the fact that whatever happened between us, I should not leave him and ghost him for that long as it hurts him too. I agreed with him because I knew that I too would not like it.

The next day, I went back to work and I realized I had a lot of work pending. Before I could proceed with anything, I had to meet David, and thank him for understanding about my leave. I was thankful to David for understanding my situation, and he had also helped Henry a lot when I had a miscarriage and ran away from home. David knew about the baby because he met me before I ran back home, and I was crying really badly.

Henry and David often met at parties and David was there for him after I left Henry. They fixed their bond after fist fights during an argument where David defended me of all the accusations we were linked with and Henry told him that he knew that nothing happened and he was just manipulated. David looked after Henry when he was constantly drunk until I came back. They had become close and Henry told me about it after I came back. I was glad that David talked him out of his doubts about us and cleared the air.

But somewhere deep down, I was still concerned about what Shelly had told me earlier. Her sleeping with Henry. And knowing how manipulative she is, I moved past all that and trusted Henry. But was the trust enough? I had no idea. I chose to trust him with all that I have because I knew how bad it hurts when someone you love does not trust you.

CHAPTER 10

Times were moving on and things were fine with Henry except for when it comes to sex. I think our love language is physical touch but we were missing something every time we tried. Henry would be needing sex and I would be zoning out during sex. The thing is, I had moved on from the incident but deep down it was still stuck with me and the scars were still hurting. I had stopped craving for sex and I had stopped needing sex. When we used to kiss, it used to give me butterflies. The moment we both were naked, I used to hold back and zone out.

We were having chaos after chaos, slowly it was draining the both of us. I was trimming his hair in the bathroom, when he received a call from an unknown number. He kept it on speaker and answered. It a call from hospital stating that Shelly was already pregnant when someone raped her. Keeping hate for her aside, a woman should not go through that pain. A woman should not cry or feel miserable, because of someone else. We both rushed to the hospital together. She was Henry's friend even if her traits were toxic. She is a woman.

As soon as we saw her, Henry talked to her and asked her what happened. She started crying and she told him that she was pregnant with his child. Now, Henry cannot remember sleeping with her and we had a fight on how could lie to me or hide things from me. It was quite shocking to know that Shelly was pregnant with Henry's child but I had not forgotten the fact that Shelly had told me before and I was a fool to trust Henry. Was me thinking that Henry is a green flag just a lie all along?

I was hurt and sad but Shelly was raped. Even though Henry denied sleeping with Shelly, she justified her pregnancy by saying that they slept only when Henry was too drunk to remember. Now how could a pregnant woman and a rape victim lie? I am a woman after all, even though I could not bring myself to ever forgive Henry. I told him to be there for her because he already made mistakes and he should not do it again. I did not want Shelly to lose the baby as she would crumble down in pieces and we didn't know what she would do to herself.

Henry was quiet for a moment and then he said that if he really made a mistake, he would be more than happy to accept the baby and be there for Shelly. I was hurting on the inside but despite being the bitch that Shelly is, I chose to agree with them and leave Henry for good. I genuinely wanted that baby to be safe, since we couldn't save ours.

We went to speak outside and I told him that we should break up. He agreed with me and apologized to me with tears rolling down his face. He told me that he does not even remember sleeping with her at all.

I told him – "She is raped and she is a victim. It would be better if we protect her rather than adding her problems on her list."

I left from there and wished him luck. I was not happy of course but I really was sad about Shelly's situation. Months passed by and I was living in my own apartment. I sometimes wondered how they are and I heard once from our mutual friend that Henry was trying and helping Shelly to recover. I had no hard feelings for them.

I had moved on from him and his life. I was focusing on myself and I had been spending more time with David due to work. We often went to party together and used to spend our evening playing games. David was helping me move on and he was there for me as a friend. A friend in need is a friend indeed.

I had my own shares of ups and downs. My mental breakdowns and my drunk rants, David was handling all of it. Now that I think of it, was David always like this with me? Was he just being a friend? Or was he just being good? Does not matter. I had given up on love.

Every time I try to build a fairytale, life falls apart.

Every time I give life or peace a chance, chaos follows.

I am not wrong, but the situation is or maybe I trusted the wrong person.

Months lead to a year, year led to another. I am now a well-known writer, travelling world and finding art. David was still around and I had no idea about Henry. I still do miss him but I am no more empty or lonely. David tried to make me feel like it's okay to get my heart broken and let it fall into pieces. He told me that without heartbreaks, life is nothing.

And it's the truth. Life is not black and white. So, was this the end of Henry and my story? I prayed that we don't let this love die young.

CHAPTER 11

In life, words have consequences. Actions have consequences. We faced ours and got separated. I had finally moved on or at least I felt like I did. I no longer felt like dying or lonely. Sometimes people change and sometimes feelings do. I was so invested in work and only hung out with David. I never had feelings for David when I was with Henry and it had been two years since I was single. I thought I would never fall for David, but two years had passed by and I no feelings for anyone.

We went to Rachel's birthday party; she is my colleague who is only 35 years old same as Katy. Katy and Rachel are best friends and Katy left the job after she had her son, a year back. I was promoted after Katy left. They both have equally helped me move on and they often told me to get laid with David as a joke because they assumed that he used to like me. We had an amazing work environment and we were all friends outside the work as well.

It was the best party I had ever been to after my breakup and I totally loved it. We were wine drunk and David didn't drink much for some reason but I was too drunk. We played cards, Uno and truth or dare and the latter was wild. Since everyone kept asking personal questions to each other, it was getting more interesting.

Katy asked Rachel when was the last time she went down on her boyfriend, she answered, "Yesterday." David asked Katy about her most embarrassing moment and she chose to drink. Most of them enjoyed drinking more than answering questions or doing the dare. It was my turn and I chose dare. Katy being herself thought that I needed to get laid so she asked me to kiss David or drink, I fumbled a little but since I was drunk and wilding, I chose to kiss David. The thing is, it would have been awkward if he did not kiss me back. But he kissed me back and I liked it. I knew I kissed a man after so long and I liked it.

Many of you who do not know how I felt at the moment will definitely call me a whore. Many of you who did not know my story will slut shame me. Social media knew the story about me and Henry, but they did not know why we had to breakup because we wanted to respect Shelly's privacy. People used to throw dirt on my name assuming I cheated on Henry because they had seen me with David. David is a billionaire and so is Henry. With all three of us having many followers on social media, we were used to being thrashed talked. But David was innocent and he was dragged. Now that I kissed David, I knew I made things more complicated for him. I was drunk and I was single, what else can you expect. Despite being famous, our privacy and family's privacy were always well maintained.

The next morning followed with hangover and memories. I knew I fucked up. I opened my social media to see pictures from the party. The videos were hilarious and of course, I finally felt happy after a long march of time. I see pictures of me and David and it got me thinking about the kiss we had. I knew it meant nothing to him but somewhere I was stuck with what if.

I never described or looked at David in any way before but the kiss made me focus on him more. Now that I had kissed him, I could not unsee his green eyes, sharp jawline, his shredded body and masculinity. I kept focusing on him more and more. Was it so bad of me to move on? Was it my fault that I developed feelings for David?

I went to work trying to focus on work and tried to avoid feelings for David. I did not want to get my heartbroken again. I did not want to be embarrassed. David could make it out that I was avoiding him. He asked my assistant to send me to his office with our new project file and I went in. David liked keeping his cabin's window closed and hanging classy painting. I was humbled real quick because he does not call anyone to his cabin and apart from his assistant, no one has entered until he called me. He asked me to close the door and take a seat. I close the door and take a seat, just as he asked me to.

He told me – "Are you ignoring me because of the kiss?"

I panic and deny quickly, trying to look cool but I got caught.

He again said – "If you are awkward and don't want to continue, you can always tell me and I will step back. What I feel for you is real and I have always loved you. I do not plan to force you into any kind of feelings." Then he comes closer to me.

I told him that I am fine with it without knowing what exactly was I talking about as I was thinking about the kiss and not hearing a single word.

He again questions- "Do you want to see if we can make things work out?"

Before I answered, I asked him if he was messing around with me because he was used to asking me out as a joke. And when he denied and said he was messing around with me. I told him that we can explore our feelings for each other.

A thirty-three years old man asking me to explore what we feel is no joke. He meant every single thing. David held my hand and started kissing me. Thankfully the door was locked and no one could see us. It was too quick and I too kissed him back.

CHAPTER 12

Kisses lead from one to another. Office sex, that was the last thing I wanted. Guess we are really good at breaking rules. While he kissed me, holding my hand, I let him take control over me and I played along. People would judge me and talk about me but the only thing that mattered to me was how I was feeling and how I felt.

David slipped his hand slowly from my thighs. He opened his tie and tied my hands so I didn't hold him. Soaking myself in sins, I let him fuck me and my pain away. Like drug, I am not able to make him stop. Bending over backwards, he slides himself inside me. My hands were still tied and he was holding my hair, while making love to me harder and harder. We forgot that we were still at work and that it had been quite some time. I moan out loud and he hushes me. He becomes meaner than demons and then gently pulls away.

"Will meet you later, I have a meeting!" - He said.

After work, the team went to try Korean hot pot and no body invited David. As much as I wanted to invite him, I did not want people to know about us. I wanted it to be a secret.

Around 12:00AM, the doorbell rang and it was night so I was hesitant to open. I received the call from David and he asked me to open the door. I rushed to open the door and he brought Blueberry cheesecake for me. We started gossiping and since we were at the early stage, I was shy. I know that after having office sex, how could I still be shy, but I was embarrassed and shy. He was the last person I would think about sleeping with.

While watching How to get away with murder, I dozed off.

Next morning, I woke up beside David in bed. I was used to waking up alone and I was shocked to see him in bed. He told me that I dozed off and he got me in bed. This was new to me. All those feelings were. I was getting butterflies and feeling loved. I went to take quick shower and David went to cook breakfast.

After breakfast, we had nothing to do since it was Sunday so David asked me if I wanted to spend some quality time with him at my place. We decided to play some games at home which led from one to another. There was pleasure in pain and pain in pleasure. Every time I hoped the love do not die young, somehow it did. I had a different feeling for David.

David wasn't so bad in bed but I couldn't feel the same way I did for Henry. However, he was wild and I loved making love with him. I often used to compare my feelings but the feelings I had developed for David were genuine and honest. He kept me happy and I felt secure.

Sometimes love change and they say good things take time, maybe David was supposed to be the person for me. I had many questions about life but only God could answer that. I am good at overthinking and I am good with letting people go since I am used to people leaving.

For a month or so, David and I kept our relation a secret and we were often busy with work and secret office sex until Rachel and the other colleagues caught us kissing near the stairs and somehow, we were the talk of the office but in a good way. As everyone was aware that David always liked me, when people around me heard about us, they news went around like a wild fire. Since David is a billionaire, I often woke up to finding our pictures circulating on newspaper and social media. I was honestly being stared by millions, but I had no fucks to give.

I was happy with David and that was all that matter to me.

I had moved on from life and left my past behind. People often thought I felt Henry because of David but he did not care about it and he wanted to respect our privacy so never told anyone about it. I was glad that he supported me and made me feel secure. You can find love and love people but loyalty is rare and hard to find.

David was one of those men who was loyal and loved me. Whether his day was good or bad, he made me feel happy and good. He was one of those who would bring the best version of themselves to support the person they love.

Do you think life would finally be a fairy tale after all?

CHAPTER 13

I always fantasized myself making love and having rough sex in a room filled with sex toys and sexual items. I was living in a small bubble and in my wild fantasy. We woman tend to have more sexual tension when we are ovulating and that is normal. I wanted him more and more during the period.

We were kissing on the bed and I was having period. Let me warn you, if you find menstruation "dirty" and "disgusting", quit reading because things are really messy here and now.

While kissing, I was on my periods, David slides his hand inside and pulls my tampon out. And like I said, I wanted him badly during that point, I let him take the lead. He was totally fine with bodily functions and he started to finger me. Things were messy, our hands, our bed and our body but we took it forward. He inserted himself inside me and we no longer knew what good or great is. I am not a saint; I am a sinner who is probably going to sin again.

I believe there are people who have done something similar before and there are people who will do it again. It is something I cannot fight against with all my heart. If you put them in right, they shouldn't hurt. Right?

There was blood and there was mess. There was blood all over the bedsheet and on him. We made rough love. We were doing missionary and the eye fuck was really good, it kept me going for long. We were just being us and not trying to justify our sexual needs. He was holding my hand, still in the same position. He sucked my breasts and started going faster and harder. It was that moment, I realized that I am wild just as anyone. He stopped and pulled out. He carried me inside shower.

We went to shower together and continued our little fantasy world.

It was rough, it was wild. It was wet and kept getting wetter. He held my neck, pushed me to the wall and kissed me. He carried me and then went he was still inside me; the shower glass was cold and we were making love.

David got a call and we realized we were in our bubble for too long to forget that we had to go and attend his sister's pre-wedding.

I wore a red gown with heart neck and slit from my upper thigh, it was hot and I looked hot. David wore a white suit with red tie to match me and he had got both our outfit customized. He was looking classy. This man really got some class.

We went to Ivy's pre-wedding and she looked absolutely gorgeous in her white and golden dress. It was embroidered with actual diamonds. As soon as we reached, she came and hugged me. She paid attention to me and it was my first time meeting his family. I wanted them to love me and I knew they did. Ivy was really sweet to me and attended me more than everyone else despite it was her wedding day.

For a week we stayed with his family and I could feel that they were very open and welcoming. Ivy also told me how David had got his heart broken before and she was glad that I loved him right and he was happy with me. She also told me how she hoped we would become a family.

The day followed with actual engagement, pre-shoots and much more. The actual wedding happened in Kensington Roof Gardens and it was a grand wedding. Ivy had also booked for a royal suit for us to stay the night in.

The wedding vows were very beautifully written. It literally got all of us in tears.

Ivy's vows –

"All my life, all I ever wanted was to love and be loved. My love for you keeps growing strong with each day passing by. There is not a single soul that can shake me from within except yours and today, when I give you my heart, I hope you shake my soul only with laughter and love. I will truly remain yours and I want you to remain mine. The work you did and the efforts you put in to make me fall in love with you even when love was the last thing, I hoped to come my way, I am grateful you came in. You came in my life and took my heart away. Away from all the heartbreaks and sadness. You took me to a fantasy that I only dreamed about. I hope we never go to sleep feeling all lonely and we know that we are never alone. We are together as one. If there will ever be anything or a spirit that make us apart, let that be a Grim reaper. You are all that I need and all that I want. With this, I take you away from everybody as my one and only husband."

Noah's vow -

"I maybe not be many things in life, but I am always a man of my word and when I give you my word, know that I mean it. I always keep it short and simple and let me keep it the same way here. I love you with all that I have and I promise to keep you safe and happy even if I have to fight against the whole world. I have only loved you and if there ever comes a day where I have to love someone else, let it be our children and no one else. With this, I take you as my wife, the only wife I would want in many different lives."

With the exchange of vows, they were happily married and it was honestly the most beautiful thing I came across.

We were very tired and we checked in the suite.

CHAPTER 14

We were never reckless and we were happy. We were wild and we were honest. David made me start my life fresh and new. He made me feel better about my past and I knew I wasn't the problem. It was the situation and time. Life is all about moving forward and I did.

From Monday to Friday, we used to be busy with our work and on Saturday and Sunday, we kept ourselves busy with each other. I came across a trending reel on Instagram, which was called Alphabet dating, so we decided to try it out for fun. We did not know how to keep our hands with ourselves. Physical touch is our love language and people around us always asked us to get a room.

We went from amusement park and apple picking to bungee jumping, circus, drive-in movie, easter egg hunt, Ferris wheel, hot tubbing, ice bar, jet ski, karaoke, live music, Movie night, nacho bar, Opera, picnic, quiz night, roller skating, star gazing, tennis, UFC match, violin concert, waterpark, X Games, yatch night to zoo trip. There was not a single thing we did not do together.

I was in love with this man. I may not have loved him the same way I loved Henry, but I was genuinely and happily in love with David.

David had lost both his parents due to cancer and was brought up by his sister, Ivy and she did a wonderful job in raising him to be a fine man. Despite him and Henry being of the same age, he did not make mistakes like Henry did. Or at least life made me see Henry's mistakes.

From bathroom floor to the dining table, from drive-in movie to hot tubbing, there was not a single place that we did not make unholy.

Love was alive in my life after all or was it just what I thought?

We dated for two years and time surely flies. We both were so busy with work and were in different countries for our book. I was in Paris for my book reading. Sadly, Paris always reminded me of Henry and the heartbreaks. He broke my heart after making promises in Paris while David made me complete after promising me in Paris.

David flew to Paris from New York for my book reading and after the event was over, we went for dinner. He proposed me with a ring. I dated Henry for three years and that only lead me with heart breaks and I dated David for two years and we were bound together like stars.

He was water and I was fire. He was whiskey and I was wine. We both enjoyed neat, but he could blend in with others. He was easy going and he was a lover. I hoped in a long march of time, we stick to one other like two souls that collide.

I have heard it's rare for people to find true love or give love another chance. I was certain with David at that moment. I loved where it was going, where life was going and where we would be going.

They say you'll know what love is when you look into someone's eyes, I found love when I looked in his eyes.

I told David of course I would marry him.

I was happy and all that mattered to me was how much in love I was with him.

When we danced through the rain, I felt quite alive again. I was lonely and I was sad, like after storm, there's calm and there's peace. David was the calm and he was the peace for me. He saw me cry and he saw me laugh. He saw me fall apart and he saw me get back together. I may not have loved him like I loved someone else but I had given him my heart. Words of love do not come easy from me but I loved him with everything that I had and will ever have.

The love that is so selfless, that is all I wished for.

David and I, we will be husband and wife.

CHAPTER 15

I woke up and uploaded a blog for David,

"To my lover,

Incase things get chaotic later, read this and remind yourself of the love, I gave you. Know that I love the way I feel when you look at me. I love the idea of us together with a bunch of holiday plans, family trips and silly little fights. You make me believe in myself and you make me believe in us. Despite everything we have done. Despite every fight. Despite every argument. I want to reach out to you and still talk to you about everything that hurts you. I want to make your heart feel at ease when you talk to me. I want to see your smile. We may be hitting rock bottom and we may be in a situation where we want to give up on us, but I know that I'll stick to you. For me, you're simply the best. I hang on every word you say, but I always hope those words are never the reason to tear us apart. The past is not my concern. The present with you is. And the future will be. You make the darkest hour seem bright. If we are destined to meet each other, we will keep meeting each other, no matter how much we run or hide. So, know that I'll be waiting for another time in case things get chaotic. You inspire the goodness in me and as long as I live, I want to hold on to that. It has

always been you and me. So, whatever it is, I want to deal with it together. You're it for me forever. I cherish the times. I cherish the love. And then there's you, I want to cherish forever. In case things get chaotic later, know that you'll always have me even when we are not together anymore."

And obviously the first person to like the blog had to be Henry. It hurt me deep down but I knew it meant nothing and he was busy with his family and kid.

David went to meet my family and asked my father if he could marry me. Every parent would want their child to be happy even if not with the person they were fond of. My parents had no idea why I ended my relation with Henry and they were still fond of Henry. But it was a fact that we all had moved on from the past. He told David that he is happy for us. David was fond of having the idea of big family since he did not have parents while growing up. I wanted to make him happy.

Ivy was more than happy to hear about me and David so she instantly flew back to London with her six months old fraternal twins named Madison and Mason. The babies were blessed with eyes like David. As soon as she reached, she handed both the twins to David and asked me to fill her in with all the details. She wanted to know how David asked me to marry him because she never imagined him asking to get married.

I told her that he purposed me in Paris after my event and she was shocked to even imagine.

Ivy reached out to my family and flew them back to London. We set a date for wedding but I did not want to rush for wedding because for the past two months, David was falling sick often. He was having anxiety and trouble breathing but he always told me he was fine and I wanted to take pre-caution for him. I asked David if we could do a simple wedding in case, he felt heartburn or dizziness again. The doctor often spoke to him regarding his health.

Ivy and I decided to do shopping for my wedding together. I did not want David to see me in my wedding dress. I wanted him to be surprised and I wanted him to be in awe. Wedding dress should be a secret from your husband after all.

Every girl dream of her wedding day and every bride deserves the to wear her dream wedding dress. It was exhausting to try so many gowns and at the end, we asked them if they could actually customize the wedding dress. I went for a sexy hourglass wedding gown. It was twenty-six pounds heavy but it was worth with all the jewelry and designs and it was a two in one dress so I could style it however I wanted to.

The gown was an off-the-shoulder lace top with semi sweetheart top covered all over with shiny beads and is in a mermaid silhouette covered with some floral patterns. It was shimmering and shining, floating into a very magnificent way. Then there was a detachable skirt made of the same material and shiny beads that made the dress go from a mermaid cut instantly to an endless train gown. The vile had to be pretty because the dress was pretty. So, I decided the tulle of the vile to be flowing till the ground and the lace at the bottom of the vile to be filled with shiny beads as my gown's top.

David and I never lived together like I did with Henry, we only used to sleep together at each other's place. We had only moved in together after we agreed to get married. After shopping, Ivy and I rushed home and found her twins and David sleeping peacefully. I realized that he could be a great father one day.

Ivy and I cooked dinner and by dinner David woke up. Noah had just reached and as soon as David woke up, he rushed to the kitchen and carried me to bed without saying anything to Noah. Ivy and her husband were feeding food to the babies and they looked at David and started laughing.

He carried me to bed while shutting the door with his leg. He kept me in bed and locked the room behind. Then he suddenly started kissing me. He wasn't gentle at all.

CHAPTER 16

I had no idea of what was going on with David. I honestly, did not. He never acted this way before but at that moment, I had no idea of anything around me except for David wanting to carry me out from kitchen and making love with me. It was fun to see him acting that way. Life was fun around him.

He was holding my both my hands tightly on the bed with his right hand, kissing me and using his left hand to pleasure me. I was pleased? Yes, I was. I had seen different sides of him and he loved me in different ways. But this side of him was different. He was rough, he was wild and he was fast. We both were making loud noises and I was shy to make Ivy and her family uncomfortable. I started moaning loud as he became harder. I couldn't resist him. I loved this man but the sex, it was getting much and much better now. He fucked me the way he never did before. He was rough and gentle before Now, he's rough, wild and dominating at the same time. I loved this version of David. I do.

David carried me to the sofa and pinned me down. Two fingers aren't enough so he used his tongue on me. One moment he is playing with me and the other moment he is inside me.

Ivy knocked the room door and told us to join them to eat because we had a busy schedule the next day.

After dinner, Ivy and I sat in the garden and we were talking about the future. She told me how different life will be with kids and family. I could imagine myself, the fact that I was pregnant before and I lost a child was hurting me still. I had moved on and life had moved on. I could imagine little versions of David and the life with them.

From what I know and what I don't, my life had crumbled down and he had picked it up for me. There was no one else who would have done the same for me. I wanted my life to be fun and happy even if the difficulties arise.

Life may or may not be a fairy tale, but David was my prince charming and he would always be.

I was hoping for a life with him and our family. I was looking forward to all that happiness and love in life. I was desperately willing to marry him.

The next morning, we all got ready for engagement and David really worked hard for my engagement ring. It was a beautiful diamond ring, the ring a woman would ever want and dream about from her fiancé.

Not everything in life is bad. Not everyone in life will hurt you.

The entire week before marriage, we were busy with our friends and family. Three days before the wedding, David was not feeling well. He was having unexplained fevers and night sweats so he went to the doctor with Ivy and Noah. I was in the mall with two of the helpers and twins to get some groceries for home.

I heard a familiar voice calling me from behind. I turn around to see Shelly calling me. The woman who I would never want to see again. She asked me if we could talk and I couldn't say no. I wanted to hear her out and hear what was left for us to talk about. As much as I hated her, I did not want to be mean to her because life happened and maybe Henry was never meant for me.

Shelly started her conversation with sorry and as soon as she said sorry, I wanted to know what she was actually sorry for. I knew she did not deserve the pain but what they did to me was wrong. I was hurting on the inside for years and no one knew except David.

I asked the helpers to get back home with the babies and the groceries and I will be back soon.

Shelly told me – "I am sorry for what happened between all of us. I have come very far in life but it still makes me guilty to think about what I did. I know you are happy now with David and you should be happy. I have seen the news and it took me long time to come and tell you that I am sorry. I think you should forgive Henry because you deserve to know the whole truth. Henry was never wrong. The truth about life is never easy to say. I am sorry that I made things worse for you and Henry. I wanted to be with Henry and marry him but the things I did to have him was wrong. I was never pregnant with Henry's child. He is innocent. The day I took Henry home, he was drunk but he kept his distance from me. I slept with his uncle Lando who told me I could date Henry if I slept with him and get pregnant and do what he tells me to. I had no idea that he wanted me to sleep with him just to get their property and money. When I got pregnant, I had nowhere to go but to blackmail Henry. I got raped while I was pregnant, I faced complications and Henry only wanted to deal with the baby and he never wanted to marry me. He got to know the truth about my pregnancy soon enough and despite knowing the fact, he helped me with everything he could for some months. Henry would come running back to you after those months, if only his mother's death did not shake him to the core. He still misses you but he is not even being himself. He was never wrong. He has always loved you"

I felt like my world fell apart.

Was I dreaming? Is life a joke? Was I having hallucinations? Why did Henry not reach out to me at all? What happened to his mother? I had questions and infact a lot of them, only Shelly could answer that. For a minute, I was blank. I forgot my anger. I forgot everything and I started questioning her.

CHAPTER 17

Shelly told me everything without missing a breath or a story. Lando would always be the problem and everyone was aware of it. When Henry caught his schemes and got to know how he used Shelly, Henry told Lando to quit doing it otherwise he will file an official police complaint against him. The same night, Henry was on his way to meet me, but he got a call from police mentioning that Isabella committed suicide. Lando went to ask Isabella for some property that belonged to Henry's father and it his father's legacy. When Isabella had denied, she was brutally raped by Lando. Henry was grieving his loss and had become an alcoholic. By the time, he fixed himself and came to look for me, I had moved on with David.

No one told me anything before because I was grieving my own loss. I felt like I was selfish to not look for him but I would not have known what to do in that situation. Was it my fault that the situation made me distant from him? Was it my mistake that he never reached out to me? Was it my fault that I never looked back? Was it my mistake Henry took two years and more to come to me and just tell me once?

All my life, I blamed him and kept blaming him but life was unfair for both of us. Life made us fall apart and life broke up into pieces. I am supposed to be married to

David in few days and now my life brought me another CHAPTER of chaos. The chaos never ends.

Was I too selfish to feel bad and not think about David? Why Henry or our friends did not tell me anything about Isabella's death?

I rushed back home and saw David in the room. I get in tears. I tell him everything and he was as shocked as me.

David asked me if I wanted to go and see Henry once. I really wanted to meet Henry and ask him why he did not tell me anything at all?

For all that I am, I was thankful to David for understanding the situation so maturely and being there to understand the pain. The truth always hurt and this truth hurt me to my core.

I rang the doorbell and as soon as Henry opened the door, he saw me and David standing there. He made a face and let us enter his house. There was a pain in his voice when he told me that he was happy for us. Most importantly, he lied. He told me that he was happy with Shelly and the baby and he is sorry that he couldn't apologize to me before.

David asked him to stop lying as I met Shelly earlier and heard everything.

Henry was pretending to be strong but he was caught so his reactions quickly changed.

I asked him why did he not tell us anything at all. David asked him if he cared so little about the friendship. We asked him way too many questions forgetting that he was in pain.

Henry asked us to chill casually.

Then he started explaining about the situation.

He told David – "I know we had become friends and you always loved Elizabeth. Despite knowing how you felt, I became friends with you because you were always genuine. I could never keep Elizabeth happy and I wanted her to be happy even if it was with you. The day you came to me asking me why I did things with Shelly, I could not give you an explanation because somewhere deep down I knew I did not fuck things up with her. I had let Elizabeth go until I could do DNA test to find out. She moved miles away from me and I was fighting my own demons. I wanted to make things all clear and right for everyone including Shelly even though she did me wrong. I never wanted any woman to feel bad. Isabella wanted me to go and propose Elizabeth and then marry her. On my way there, I lost my mother."

He falls in tears and he continues.

"After losing my mother, I was in pain and I had become an alcoholic. It took me time to detox myself and by that time, it took me years. I heard the news that you both were dating and I wished nothing but best. Yes, I could have come to both of you, but I did not. Yes, I could have made things right but you both had moved on. I wanted both of you to be happy and married. If there is anything in life, I ever wanted more than anything, it's you and your happiness. My feelings stay the same. I still love you but I want you to be happy and I hope you both get married."

After hearing him, I go blank and it hurts me to think that I still feel for him and it never changed.

CHAPTER 18

I could not betray David. I said it before and I would say it again, I was genuine with him and I loved him. I may not have loved him the same way I loved Henry but I did not want to leave him or hurt him. I was so clueless and helpless. It's not that easy with things that were going on, I wanted to stay with David because life was never on our side for me and Henry. Whenever I saw families and kids, I had imagined only Henry until I was to be married to David. I liked the idea of marrying David and having family with him until my past unfolded the truth.

David understood my pain and he comforted me as well.

I chose to get married to David as I could not be selfish because of my past and I did love him.

We woke up early for the wedding and got ready. I was feeling quite uneasy because that was not how I expected life to be. I was wearing everything as planning and David looked stunning. My father walked me to the aisle. David held my hand and it was time for our vows.

I fumble with my words and being – "I may not promise you the world, but I.."

Then I stay silent for few minutes. I look at David and he is looking at me. I was having anxiety and panic attacks. He gets me a glass of water and then he asks the priest if he can take the vow first.

David's vow - "Life can take me many places and wherever I go, I will search for you. My eyes cannot see you unhappy, my eyes cannot see you sad and my eyes cannot see you cry. When I told you, I would bring you the world and I will give it to you, I meant it. Even if bringing the world to you means breaking my own heart. I love you so much that I cannot see you unhappy. All my life, I have only imagined myself marrying one woman and that woman is you. Life may not have been all moon and stars. There was storm and there was chaos. There was love and there was art. You distract me from a lot of things I do in life, including my work but I seem to be a lot more distracted without you. May everyone find a woman in their life as gentle and as sweet as you. Maybe we are meant to be in another life but not this, I cannot take you as my wife in this life because I want to see you happy."

Everyone looked at David and I was as shocked as they were wondering what had happened. I was wondering what changed.

David asked Henry to come up said to me - "I know years passed away; life went on. Things changed and situation changed. It was no one's fault. I see that you both love each other the same way. The thing is I want to marry you but I want your love completely and you do not love me the way you love Henry. I have seen you both look at each other. I have seen you both cry for each other. I know that you would be better and happy together.

David turns towards Henry and said, - "If you do not keep her happy and move mountains for her, I will come and make sure you both get divorced the next time. For this life, she is yours and from another life, I will make her all mine."

How can someone be so selfless? How can someone keep other before themselves?

David asked us to get married with each other and I was quite hesitant to rush things then Ivy came to talk some sense to me and told me that people do not get chance for true love twice. She tells me to go and grab the chance while I still can.

Henry tells me that he was sorry that he fucked up many times but he will work on it and he will make sure things go properly the next time.

While I was debating with my thoughts, I got a call from David's doctor regarding his reports. I loved David, for a fact so after hearing about the report, I just couldn't get myself to be married to Henry on the same day.

I told Henry that I will call the wedding off because I was not quite ready to marry him yet and David was not well. We are supposed to be there for him as he has cancer.

Ivy interrupts me by saying that the report came early morning and everyone is already aware about the cancer. As much as she is sad about his cancer, David wants me to be happy and married to Henry.

I felt like everyone was putting a lot of pressure on me. I felt like I needed space.

David asked me to calm myself and get married to Henry.

Henry told me that he would help me look after David along with me and he understands my feelings for him.

With that, I choose to marry Henry.

CHAPTER 19

We took fifteen minutes break to think through and David kept telling me that there would always be something between me and Henry that I will never be able to forget. It was a fact. My relationship with Henry was on and off but it kept revolving around him. I was not exactly happy with Henry at that time, but deep down, I knew I would not be happy without him. Isabella would be happy to know or see him right now.

As much as I was in love with Henry, I was also worried about David's health. Everyone was asking me to go ahead with the wedding so I decided to go with it. After all my feelings were stronger for Henry.

I told Henry that I would go ahead with the wedding only if he lets me take care of David until he recovers from cancer and I cannot be selfish because he was always selfless.

When Henry agreed and said that he would want the same. We get back to the wedding.

The gown I was supposed to wear and get married to David turned out to be the wedding gown that I am wearing and getting married to Henry. I felt guilty for David's situation but he kept insisting that I get married to Henry.

This time, David along with my father walks me to the aisle and I was getting married.

My vows - *"I know now that what we have transcends and is a much deeper soul connection. We have been at our ugliest and most vulnerable times with each other. We are chaos and we are peace at the same time. This is the first of many hard decisions we made together as a team and there will be many more we need to make as one. David might have got us back together, but sticking together is entirely on our hands. We keep circling around and coming back to each other for more. I hope every time we fight, we come back to each other. May you never lose you path or get lost while searching for me. Out of all the people you've met in your life, you chose me and out of all the places you've visited, you ended up here again. Life wasn't a bloody fairytale with you and it will never be because life is never easy, but let's get ready for one hell of a ride and make it worthwhile. I hope you support me and love me the way you did before. I had always loved you and no matter how far I go in life; life brings me back to you. From losing what we valued the most to finding love in what we value, we came back. I hope from here and now, life takes a different path for us and we stay happy together, forever and always. We faced obstacles which maybe harder than others and we will keep our lessons learned. With this, I, Elizabeth, take you, Henry, to be my husband, my friend, my family and my love. When you need help and care, I will stand right there for you. And when you do the same for me, which I know you will, I will love you even more. For the rest of my life, I am yours. Please don't let the love die young."*

Henry's vows - *"You've shown me more love than I've ever known while I did not even know what love felt like and when I needed it. I am lucky to stand here and to be able to call you mine after everything that happened and where life led us. They say God has better plans than ours and God did have better plans for us. This would not be possible without David and I hope we never let him down. You have understood me and accepted me in ways where no one ever has. I can show you versions of me that I cannot even think of showing someone else. I will always be your protector and confidante. I will be responsible for making sure your every need is met and every want is reached. I will make sure that every dream of yours are lived. With love in my heart, I vow to be always by your side until my last breath. There was no woman before you and there will be no woman after you except if you are giving me a daughter. I was drawn towards you from the moment we met and I will be the same even if death do us apart. For all that I am and all that I will every be, I am yours and I want to be your husband. With this, I, Henry, take you, Elizabeth as my wife. I love you and I will not let the love die young"*

We exchanged our rings and kissed.

Henry and I just got married.

CHAPTER 20

Henry and I decided not to go away for the honeymoon until David recovers and David was struggling for four months with chemotherapy and other medical activities. We were constantly with him and helping him recover. His ex-girlfriend heard the news about his cancer and came back rushing to see him from Australia. Somewhere deep down, he found his love back.

Nobody really knows how to fight cancer except for the patient and doctors and Henry often went to church to pray for David, but they say that your life and fate is entirely on God's hand. He was one of the purest souls, and it was difficult for us to see him leave the world. David deserved better things in life. He surely did. I had loved him and somewhere deep down I still do.

Months later I published a book called – "Holding my heart from heaven."

"To David,

The one who is holding my heart from heaven. I know you're not going to read this and you'll never know how I feel or how I felt. But I hope you know and you can see. Life was beautiful with you, every second was and when you left, it was gloomy. Took me time to move on but you are still holding your place. Won't say it took me ages to be happy again, but it was difficult. And even now when I think about you, it still aches. I am quite happy now and hope you are happy up there too. I hope you look at me and can see everything you wanted me to be. Just want to make you proud and not break you down. I keep looking for you everywhere, but I know I won't get the same friendship anywhere else. I want to tell you so many things about my life and how is it going and I bet you're looking. There are a lot of things I can't talk about with anyone else except you. Many things I want to do, but you aren't there. That emptiness and the voids can never be filled with anyone's presence. And if I could ask God for one thing, I would ask him to let you be in peace because you deserve it. I would love to hear your voice one last time. I would love to see you one last time. Been months since you left us and that guilt of not being able to help you when we all tried still holds me up at night. You're gone but never forgotten. Always in our memories. It was hard to say goodbye, looking at your body. A person video calling me a day before and talking about how he wanted to travel the world again was lying on the ground. Not a single sound. Not a single smile was visible. Time heals the wounds now, but the hearts still broken. I think about you and wonder how could you be so bright, even until the end. Your death did us apart, but never by heart. No one knows why did it happen to you. And one thing for sure, we loved you and we still do. And by "we", I mean your family, your friend and me. You're not here to tell me where am I going wrong. You're not here to guide me. Loving you was the hardest because I had to let you go in a way where I would never see you again. I'm writing this to you. Remembering those memories. Remembering the memories and love. Remembering it is easy while letting go wasn't. You are still holding my heart from heaven. I still got the same love for you. You'll always be a part of who I am right now. You'll never be someone I'll get over. You deserved more than this world could give you. You deserved love and you deserved happiness. I miss your smile. I miss your talks. I miss everything you used to do for me. Especially, I miss you. You'll always have that piece of my heart."

And the book continued.

Henry helped me publish the book.

Henry and I lived together and we were happy. Was life a fairytale? No, it was not. Life could not be more twisted than this.

CHAPTER 21

We were grieving from David's loss and before David passed away, I had found out that I was once again pregnant. One thing I knew for sure, it was not Henry's child.

I could not bring myself to tell neither David nor Henry about my pregnancy. David was focused on his chemotherapy and I did not want Henry to be responsible for what was not his. After marrying Henry, we kept our hands to ourselves because we needed time to move forward. I pushed him away every time he tried to come close to me. And that is how I know the baby was not his.

Henry supported me with everything I did and my baby bump was slowly visible. I was so afraid of being caught and had no explanations. Henry had promised to support me and I knew he would support me but I did not want to burden him.

I insisted Henry to give me a divorce saying I did not feel the same kind of love for him. He assumed that I was grieving from the loss so he agreed to give me space but he would not divorce me. I loved him with all that I was.

Having no choice left with me, I signed a divorce paper and left from London forever. I knew this would be hard for Henry and life would be hard for me to raise a baby alone.

I left a letter to Henry and told him how grateful I was to be loved by him. I told him I would never marry anyone else apart from him, I knew it was selfish of me but I thought that was the best for the baby.

Life was really not in our favor. I told my best friends everything about the baby and how I did not want to tell Henry, Carol and Mia helped me settle down in Amsterdam. There was no mountain, I would not move for Henry but I did not want to make him responsible for what was never his. I wanted to take care of the baby myself because I owed it to David and it was his.

Henry had no idea about me and the baby. After shifting in Amsterdam, I always assumed that Henry must have thought I left for good. I assumed he hated me.

I had no idea of him. I had deleted all my social media and I had quit writing. I was not in touch with my family either. I used to call them only on their birthdays and vacations. They had no idea about the baby either, I had blocked Henry's calls and messages. I used to miss him and I often felt like calling him but I was scared of telling him.

Life went on and I soon gave birth to a son, the little Dilan. He resembled his father more than me. I used to cry myself to sleep missing Henry sometimes and I was guilty that I left. I had promised him forever when I could not give him forever. After all, the child was more important for me.

I thought I was doing it right in life, but it was difficult to raise a child. Dilan grew up quickly and it did not feel like years. I had accepted my life alone but Dilan was in kindergarten when he started questioning me about his father. When all the kids had both their parents, he was curious to know about his father. It used to break my heart every time he used to ask me.

How am I supposed to tell a four-year-old that his father died? How am I supposed to tell a baby that I was never married to his father? How am I supposed to tell that child that he had a different father?

I often told Dilan that his father is working hard to send him gifts.

One day, Dilan was playing in the guest room and my phone was with him, a small child with no idea of who he is answering to picked up the call and told a number where he was living. As soon as I hear him, I took the phone from him and answered. But the call got disconnected, so I did not pay much attention to it.

After that I was well aware that Dilan should not be trusted with a phone because he was just a baby and I had not told anyone else apart from my best friends.

Many thoughts kept running on my mind and I thought that it was time for me to tell my family about the baby.

So, I went to America with Dilan. As soon as I reached America, I went to tell my family about Dilan. Out of many things, Dilan would have wanted in life, I knew he wanted a family not only his mother. I wanted him to know what having a family feels like. I have made many mistakes and I knew I should have told Henry about it. I did what I felt was right for him but maybe he would have accepted the fact and loved me the same way.

Would Henry be fine knowing the truth? Or did he already move on in life?

Was life always supposed to be this complicated? Or was I complicating my life more than it already was?

CHAPTER 22

I travelled back to America after years and I really loved being back. No one had any idea of what I was doing in life now, all they knew was that I was alive.

I rang the doorbell and my father was shocked to see me carrying a child. I let Dilan play with Bella for some time. Bella was at my father's place before I started dating David and I had left Henry due to Shelly.

I had to tell my father about Dilan eventually and everything that happened over the years. He was shocked but he was sad about the fact that I did not tell him or Henry anything at all.

My father told me that Henry kept looking for me and is still looking for me. He handed me some letters from Henry and asked me why I could think that this man would not support me. When I tried to explain him how I did not want to burden him with someone else's child. He looked at me and made a face of disbelief.

Dilan met his grandfather for the first time and the curiosity of the child made him ask his grandfather about his father and why his father never came to meet him.

My father replied – "Your father is a very busy man and he was sick, he will come to meet you when he is healthy."

The poor child believed it and kept playing with Bella.

We stayed in America for a week and my father made sure that Dilan gets a family time.

I think I was selfish to not talk to my family or Henry about the baby and we are humans, we let our assumption and thoughts win.

I always held my wedding vows close to my heart but I did break many. I broke Henry's heart and I broke Dilan's heart more than anyone. He was just a child after all.

I was not ready to read Henry's letters quite yet because I was not prepared and I would get a mental breakdown once again. Life went on but my life keeps circling back to him. There was not a single night where I slept peacefully or with no tears. My little baby had seen me cry and in pain.

I tried everything in life to avoid Henry but why do I keep missing him? Why does my life keep circling back to him?

Dilan was happy to finally to around my brother and my father. He insisted we take Bella to Amsterdam and we did.

My art gallery and my small café was doing well in Amsterdam but I missed writing book. I was desperately to write again. I started writing my book again but I did not want Henry to know where I was living, so I did not feel the need to publish it.

With a very heavy heart, I started reading letters that Henry wrote to me.

CHAPTER 23

"Dear Elizabeth,

If you are reading this, know that I have been searching for you everywhere I go and you are nowhere to be found. Your family and your friends have no idea where you and I am desperate to find you.

I am living in mental hell and wondering where did I go wrong.

If I have done something to make you feel bad, tell me or call me. I have sent your over four thousand voice mails and endless missed call yet I am not able to connect with you.

If I have loved you less, I will love you more. Please contact me."

How do I tell him it was not his fault? How do I tell him I fucked up? How do I tell him that I could not bring myself to tell him how I felt?

Another letter:

"Dear Elizabeth,

It has been months since I last heard your voice and I understand if you take your space, but leaving is never the solution for life. I tried to contact every single person we have ever known to find out about you yet no one knows. Your friends are not ready to help me out and I feel like I am drowning myself.

I cannot imagine this life without you. Out of all the art in the museum, my favorite will always remain to be you.

I hope you understand that I am ready to talk to you and fix things."

It shattered my heart.

Whenever I see him sad, I feel sad. I knew I messed things for us but I had no idea of how to fix the mess.

I read all his letters and the love remained the same. He was desperate to hear back from me as much as I was desperate to tell him. I just did not know how to.

Out of all the letters, my favorite was:

"Dear Elizabeth,

I have written many letters to you and I know you have not read it yet. And when you know, please come back to me. I will be waiting for you. If I have done something wrong, correct me. If you have done something wrong, tell me, so we can fix things and stick to one another just like our vows.

My heart is crying in pain of memories of you and my soul is creating storm in fear of losing you. I know I was not always easy; I have been difficult. I know I have been a pain, but I never meant to harm you in any other way.

When you said life is not always a fantasy, I knew whether life would be a fantasy or reality, I would love you and keep waiting for you. Like I am waiting for you now. I have been going crazy trying to search for you. I still have not signed the divorced papers yet because we are bound together like stars. I am waiting for you and I know you are waiting for me too,

I have hope in destiny and our destiny collides. We keep coming back to each other to help each other heal. I never knew what love truly is until I met you, Elizabeth. You are the one I want from morning till night.

I will keep waiting for you until I turn old and cranky.

Truly yours,

Henry."

I felt like calling Henry and meeting him as quickly as possible but I did not. I controlled my feelings to think it clear. Little does he know how I am breaking every time I think about you. Little does he know that I am still haunted by the memories of us. Little does he know it breaks my heart to break his heart. Little does he know I still love him.

I may no longer live and turn into ashes but my love for him will remain the same.

I am trying to make things right for Dilan pieces my pieces but how can I be selfish to make Henry a father of someone else's child.

CHAPTER 24

Out of all the love, I would find in this world, I would not be able to find love like his. Even if something as vast and scattered as the stars were to fall apart, every piece would come together to form us.

From when I was in my twenties to now when I am in my thirties, I have loved him and, in my head, it has always been him. I tried rewriting this love many times but if it is not him who I end up with, I get my heart broken multiple times.

He was a dream to me, the dream I can never sell. The dream that I always wanted to keep dreaming. I know I could love him better than I do.

Dilan went for school camping and I wanted to spend some time alone, I was constantly getting drunk. Amsterdam was pretty chill and I was in the bar getting wasted and dancing with some stranger. I was so drunk that I felt like I was hallucinating and I kissed a man, who looked like Henry. I imagined the person to be him and I was so drunk that I could only see him face.

I made out with that person and one thing led to another. I was vulnerable and drunk and I left things happen. I was too drunk to stop myself and I was mentally sober enough to know that it was not Henry.

The man kissed me and as far as I remember that we were still kissing until I reached his room. He carried me to his bed and kissed me again. His hand went to touch me where I wanted to be touched and I wanted to be loved. I had been lonely for years, I wanted to be loved mentally and physically. I had my needs. I went along with the person imagining it to be Henry.

I was drunk but I know every single detail of where this man touched me. He touched my soul piercing kisses through my skin. He made me feel like vulnerable was honest and he made me feel like it was okay not to be okay.

He used his fingers and tongue to pleasure me and made me every single movement slowly and deep. I knew the consequences would be embarrassing the next day but I did it anyway.

They say that the drunk version of you is where you meet the slutty version of yourself. I was being a slut because I was drunk and I know nothing can justify that.

He went inside me and fucked me exactly like Henry and I started sobbing. I don't remember anything after that.

The next morning, I woke up with hangover and I knew I had fucked it up and I was good at fucking things for myself. I turned around to see the man I was sleeping with before I could run from there and swore to never do it again. I see Henry sleeping next to me. I was as shocked as anyone would be. I thought it was just my assumption and I was hallucinating.

"Henry?" I shout.

How did he come here? How did he know about me? How did he meet me? I was confused.

He opens his eyes slowly and pulls me closer to him.

"Get some sleep, we will talk later." - He said.

I lay down as he told me to and was still wondering.

We fall asleep in his hotel for more than five hours and when we both wake up, I asked him many questions and he told me he would answer one by one.

Henry told me he forced Mia and Carol to give my phone number and when he called a boy picked up. He panicked and he asked them to tell him everything they know. He was aware about my situation and why he left me. He took time to think what he should do and asked Carol and Mia not to tell me anything. He told me that know why I did what I did and he was understands but he would have just accepted Dilan.

I told him that I did not want to burden him with responsibilities and Henry insisted that we raise him together.

Henry said - "Instead of running away and assuming I would not be there to support you, you could have told me and we could have planned how to raise him together. I may not be David and he may not be my own child. I would raise him like my own. I may not be a perfect father but at least I would have loved him like I would have loved our own child. Instead of making Dilan fatherless and lonely, let's work on being a good parent to him."

After having a conversation with Henry, it also made me realize, we would have been doing better if I had told him about Dilan instead of running away.

I went back to my house and Henry checked out from hotel and we thought of telling Dilan about Henry together and let Dilan meet his father. We chose to keep it a secret from Dilan about David.

Until Dilan was back, Henry and I was busy with going on dates and visiting places.

When I looked at Henry naked, I could see the changes in his body. He had also made a tattoo, "I will love you even when life is no fairytale, please don't let the love die young."

His tattoo made me remember and relive every single moment from the first day we met till the time we got married. I chose to marry this man and vowed that I would never let our love die young. I know I would always be his and he would always be mine.

I do not know if life would be happily ever after but from this point, I would never leave his side. Once Dilan was back, we told him Henry is his father and swore to keep David's story away from Dilan.

CHAPTER 25

We had our fair share of love and war and life always made us go through battles. Despite everything we have been through, we never changed,

I cannot promise him certain things in life, but I promise not to leave his side from here and now. Henry and I decided to get married and retake our vows again despite being married. He never signed the divorce papers.

While Bella carried our rings and Dilan helped me walk the aisle along with my father, we all were happy and, in the end, it was all that mattered to me. Life would have been completely different without Henry by my side. I was grateful to be his and he was grateful to be mine.

He looks at me like I am an art and it makes my heart race. He loves me like I am delicate and I want to love him more. All my life, it was him all along.

I tried doing all that I could, in the end, it's useless and I am empty without him. If I say, I don't love him, it is a lie. I cannot play games and put my heart on line because my heart beats faster only for him. I am not the kind of woman who will go through hell just to let him go.

Henry has always set the bar above the moon for me. He is everything I ever wanted and I would lose myself than lose him. The smiles on my face when he got me flowers, read me books or just talk to me something money could not buy.

For better or for worse, I am glad Henry came back to me and he keeps coming back to me. I don't want to be in my forties or fifties regretting anything in life or living with the memories of us. We were young and in love when we did not know better. We were growing and learning when we were getting together. Things change when you love a person and put all the that you have to make things go wrong.

When he looks at me in my eyes and says he loves me, it still makes my heart flutter. He gives me reasons to stay and love him. I know I cannot unlove him, ever. I hated myself for justifying leaving him because I felt like I would be a burden to him.

The versions of him that I had seen, I know he is all mine. My one and only, Henry.

Till death do us apart, I will not let the love die young. I promise, I only love him.

www.ingramcontent.com/pod-product-compliance
Lightning Source LLC
La Vergne TN
LVHW041619070526
838199LV00052B/3201